For our children,
Violette, Sadee, Ryan Kaya, and Mason,
and our Maui community

This book belongs to: _____

Are you ready to find the Magical Hawaiian Rainbow?

Magical
Hawaiian Rainbow
Adventure through Lāhainā

Written by Shauvon Young
Illustrated by Tioni Acain

On an island in the middle of the vast Pacific Ocean with sun-kissed palm trees, turquoise waters, and adventure at every bend lives a courageous girl named Keona. Keona's tutu, Kealoha, shares an enchanting story about a magical rainbow. "It's brightly colored in the sky. Its vivid glow catches every eye. It's the Magical Hawaiian Rainbow!"

With Keona's eyes wide with enthusiasm and a joyful grin, she knows her adventurous spirit is ready to begin.

"This is the day the Lord has made; let us rejoice and be glad in it."
Psalm 118:24

In search for someone to join her exciting quest, Keona chooses her best friend. She knows it is best. "Aloha, Leilani, would you like to join me on an adventure to find the Magical Hawaiian Rainbow?"

"I would love to,'ae," exclaims Leilani. "Let's find something new, explore the ocean blue, and I'll gladly climb the highest peak with you!"

"Blessed is she who has believed that the Lord would fulfill his promises to her!"
Luke 1:45

They pack a small bag with sweets and treats, oh, my, plenty to eat! They jump in Tutu's boat with the pursuit of hope. With their hearts full of excitement, their adventure is taking flight. Their future is looking bright!

"The Lord will guide you always..."
Isaiah 58:11

Off they go! As they row, row, row, it's time to embark on their grand adventure to find the legendary rainbow!

"For we live by faith, not by sight."
2 Corinthians 5:7

With spirits shining bright, the keiki are ready for a wondrous sight. "Let's explore and search for signs of the Magical Hawaiian Rainbow," Keona says excitedly as their boat draws near the shore.

"Ask and it will be given to you; seek and you will find..."
Matthew 7:7

"We're here! We're here! I can feel we're so near," Leilani says, beaming with joy. Stepping off their boat, they arrive at the harbor of a charming town called Lāhainā on their neighboring island of Maui. The girls are overjoyed! Their smiles are bright and wide, like a rainbow in the sky.

"If you believe, you will receive whatever you ask for in prayer."
Matthew 21:22

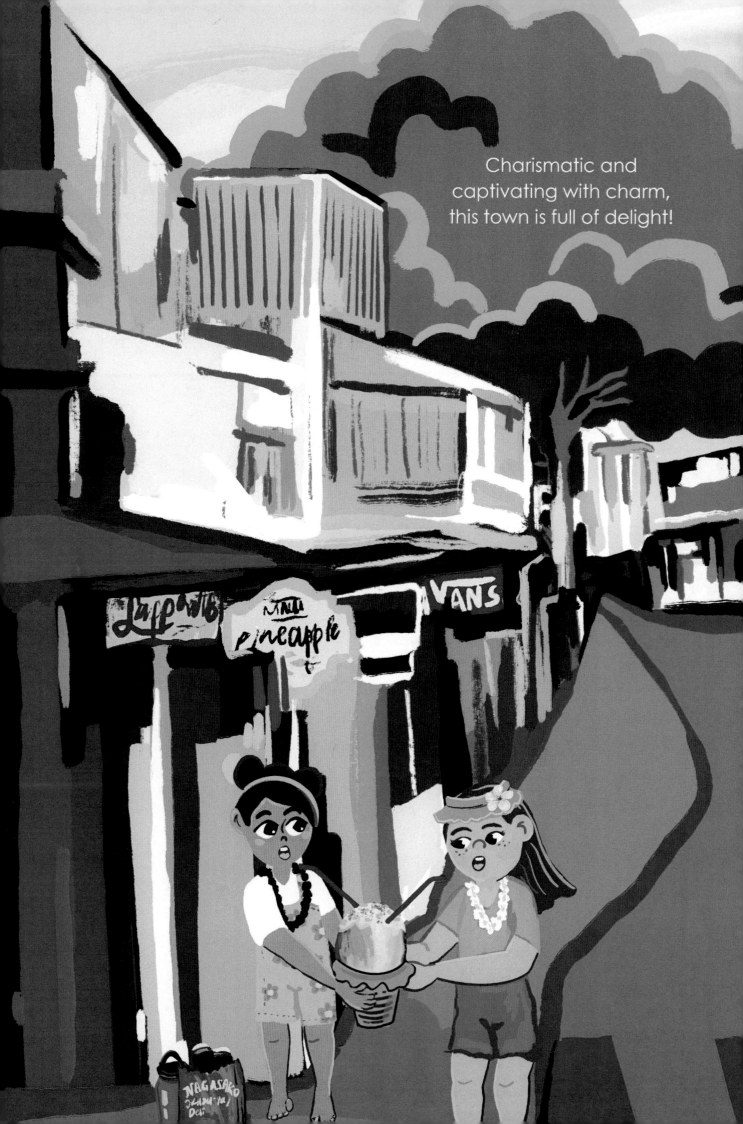

Charismatic and captivating with charm, this town is full of delight!

"And we know that in all things God works
for the good of those who love him..."
Romans 8:28

While thirsty for a sweet treat,
although the 'elua keiki have food
packed, they're in paradise.
Surely they'll have a shave ice!

Continuing down Front Street with wonder in their eyes, they're set for an awe-inspiring surprise... "Wait! Do you hear that?" Keona wonders.

"In their hearts humans plan their course, but the Lord establishes their steps."
Proverbs 16:9

Sounds of cheerful ukulele music and an incredible aroma of tropical flowers fill the air with delight.

"It's a hula show!" Keona says excitedly as they join in the fun. Immersed in the Hawaiian sound, feeling the islands' magic all around, amazed at how the hālau blend wisdom and culture within their hula dance and share aloha from their hearts.

"Let them praise his name with dancing..."
Psalm 149:3

"...Love one another as
I have loved you."
John 15:12

Filled with so much joy, the keiki are losing all track of time.
"What time is it? In a hurry we must go, chasing the ānuenue
that brightly glows!" Leilani says in a rush.

They share a heartfelt moment of appreciation and
eagerly continue on their adventure.

"I can do all this through him who gives me strength."
Philippians 4:13

After wandering a considerable distance with joyful persistence, a sense of discouragement starts to settle in. The keiki wonder if they will ever find the rainbow still hidden from sight.

"Let's sit under this banyan tree," Keona says as she
wipes sweat from her brow. "I'm feeling wela and
this beautiful tree can provide plenty of shade for
us to rest, then we can continue on our quest."

Feeling the warmth of the afternoon sun, the girls feel the day is just about done. "We can't give up. We can do this!" insists Keona. "I believe my tutu's stories and Ke Akua will show us the way to the rainbow. Let's go search for its glow!"

"Trust in the Lord with all your heart..."
Proverbs 3:5

Forging ahead, bright and carefree, the keiki are pleasantly surprised by what they see. "This is the Waiola Church," Keona recalls. "My tutu has shared many stories of our ancestors coming here. It's two hundred years old and very special!"

"For where two or three gather in my name, there am I with them."
Matthew 18:20

"I praise you because I am fearfully and wonderfully made; your works are wonderful, I know that full well."
Psalm 139:14

Their laughter and joy fill the air! They dance hand-in-hand without a care, feeling so grateful for this delightful adventure.

"Mahalo nui, Leilani, for joining me on this adventure. I'm grateful to call you my best friend," Keona says with a big smile.

"Me too, and although we have yet to see the ānuenue, I've had such a magical time exploring with you," Leilani says.
"The magic is just having a great friend like you!"

"A friend loves at all times..."
Proverbs 17:17

Although Keona's heart remains set on finding the Magical Hawaiian Rainbow, she begins to realize maybe her tutu's story holds a meaning beyond its radiant glow.

"Aha!" Leilani gasps with excitement. "Your tutu's story must be about our journey together and the magical moments we're sharing. Maybe this is what the Magical Hawaiian Rainbow is about!"

"We love because he first loved us."
1 John 4:19

"Your word is a lamp for my feet, a light on my path."
Psalm 119:105

With raindrops tapping on their foreheads and the grand mountains in view, something catches Leilani's sight—a beautiful glow shining bright.

With the glow getting brighter with each step, they each quicken their pace, their hearts brimming with excitement!

At last, its vibrant colors putting on a show, arching gracefully with a radiant glow, as if it's kissing the mountains, bridging the Heavens to the earth.

"We did it!" Keona cheers. "We found it, and it's even more magical than I could have ever imagined!" Captivated by its sheer beauty, Leilani gushes, "It's the most beautiful ānuenue I have ever seen!"

"I have set my rainbow in the clouds, and it will be the sign of the covenant between me and the earth."
Genesis 9:13

Each takes off her lei and lays it on the mountain's display as a symbol of gratitude and aloha, realizing in this moment that as beautiful as the rainbow is, the true magic is the beauty of their friendship.

"Give thanks to the Lord, for he is good; his love endures forever."
Psalm 107:1

"I am the light of the world. Whoever follows me will never walk in darkness, but will have the light of life."
John 8:12

Painting the sky with colors so bright the Magical Hawaiian Rainbow starts to fade out of sight.

The keiki's hearts are overjoyed with pure delight, enjoying the captivating rainbow shinning bright, knowing their special friendship and wonderful adventure they share are truly magical all on its own.

"The Lord is trustworthy in all he promises and faithful in all he does."
Psalm 145:13

"Let them give glory to the Lord and proclaim his praise in the islands."
Isaiah 42:12

Locations referenced in illustrations

ILLUSTRATIONS LISTED IN ORDER OF APPEARANCE

Lāhainā boat harbor

The Pioneer Inn

Lāhainā Lighthouse

Old Lāhainā Courthouse

Front Street, Lāhainā

Historic Baldwin Home Museum

Front Street Banyan Tree

Lāhainā's Old Fort

King Kamehameha III Elementary School

Waiola Church

Pioneer Mill Smokestack

Lāhainā coastline

West Maui Mountains

Maui island

Did you find all the hidden hearts?

Embark on your own adventure to discover a hidden ♡ within every illustration!

Hawaiian language from the book

MAIN CHARACTERS

Keona: God's gracious gift

Leilani: Heavenly garland of flower

Kealoha: The loved one

HAWAIIAN WORDS

Keiki: Children

'Elua keiki: Two children

Tutu: Grandma

Aloha: "Hello" and "goodbye" and also so much more: it's sharing kindness, compassion, gratitude, and love while greeting one another with aloha spirit

'Ae: Yes

Mahalo nui: Thank you very much

Ke Akua: God

Hula: Hawaiian dance

Hālau: A group of hula dancers; a school or group dedicated to learning and performing hula

Ānuenue: Rainbow

A special dedication note

This children's story is dedicated to all of the Lāhainā community: na keiki, ʻohanas, kūpuna, business owners, beloved pets, and everyone who calls Lāhainā home. As well as to our whole Maui community and our ʻohanas, this book is from our hearts to all of yours.

With Lāhainā being very close to both of our hearts, we wanted to make this children's book to uplift our community in remembrance of Lāhainā after the devastating Maui wildfires of 2023. We created this passion project with the goal in mind to help preserve for children and families the legacy of Lāhainā's rich history and beauty for generations to come.

Additionally, we aspired to create something special that could be cherished by children all over the world, so that they can always view beautiful Lāhainā in the illustrations. We want this story to take families through different historical locations pre the Maui wildfires, to showcase the Hawaiian culture, and to imbue readers with the aloha spirit as they learn about the importance of friendship, community, and treasuring special moments.

We want our readers to feel that at any time they can open this book and feel like they are right there journeying through charming Lāhainā, which we all hold so dear to our hearts. We hope you feel the aloha and love we have poured into this book for all of you.

With much aloha,
Shauvon & Tioni

About the Author: SHAUVON YOUNG

Shauvon Young is a passionate writer with a deep love for children's books. As a devoted mother, she understands the importance of storytelling in a child's development. With a life immersed on Maui, she has created a profound connection to the community and culture.

Shauvon embarked on her journey as a children's book author to share heartwarming stories that seamlessly combine imagination and education, transporting readers to imaginary worlds while keeping the locations in her stories real so that readers can learn about valuable history and culture while delighting in the joy of reading. She aims to captivate both children and adults alike.

After studying journalism at Sacramento State University, Shauvon honed her writing skills through various mediums, bringing stories to life for readers of all ages. She has always loved to write and tell stories, her favorite by far being children's stories.

Shauvon also supports the Maui community and nonprofits through various methods within her continued philanthropist efforts. She finds joy in spending beach time with her family and dancing hula with her hālau.

Through her writing, Shauvon aims to foster a love for literature in children, hoping to inspire young readers, ignite their imaginations while learning about history and culture, and empower them to dream BIG!

About the Illustrator: TIONI ACAIN

Tioni Acain is an artist hailing from the beautiful island of Maui, Hawaii. Her passion lies in acrylic paintings that capture the wonders of this paradise she calls home. Drawing inspiration from the landscapes and creatures around her, she aims to showcase their beauty through her unique perspective.

With each stroke of paint on canvas, Tioni creates a symphony of colors that evoke a sense of natural movement. Look closely at each piece and you'll discover a hidden heart, symbolizing her deep love for art.

She owes much gratitude to Janet Sato for nurturing her artistic talent during high school. Alongside talented artists like Kirk Kurokawa and Philip Sabado, she contributed to a cultural mural showcased at the Ritz-Carlton Maui.

In 2019, amidst a successful corporate career as an area manager, Tioni won the prestigious 31st Lāhainā Art Society annual poster contest with her acrylic masterpiece "West Maui Lāhainā." It became a limited edition 2020 poster cherished by art enthusiasts everywhere.

While she excelled in developing future leaders in business, creating art has remained her true calling.

artbytioni.com
@art_bytioni
Maui, Hawaii